Hate Inexorable

by

Mike Duke

Copyright ©2018 by Mike Duke

All rights reserved. No part of this book may be used or reproduced by any means, graphic, electronic, or mechanical, including photocopying, recording, taping or by any information storage retrieval system without the written permission of the publisher except in the case of brief quotations embodied in critical articles and reviews.

This is a work of fiction. All the characters, names, incidents, organizations, and dialogue in this novel are either the products of the author's imagination or are used fictitiously.

Acknowledgments

I want to express my sincere thanks to those beta readers who gave me critical feedback which helped make this story a powerful kick in the gut. Big shout out to Lisa Lee Tone (who also did an outstanding job of editing the final version), Lisa Swearengin, Tommy Clark, Craig Massey, Kevin Kennedy, and William Holloway.

It was 8:30 am on a Monday morning when Kendall pulled into a spot in the large public parking lot facing Pacific Ave. He and Krystal got ready for the family trip to the beach earlier than planned after their thirteen-month-old son, Matthew, had woken up well before his normal time.

Kendall didn't mind. He was glad to arrive early before the Memorial Day crowd laid siege to the shoreline. He and Matthew could stake their claim to an area big enough to build a sand castle with a moat and everything. They wouldn't have to compete for space among the waves so much, either.

Plus, we'll have our fill of fun before the sun gets high enough to start scorching us red as lobsters, Kendall thought as he put the gold Lincoln Mark VIII in park.

It was a bit old, but the mileage was low. Kendall didn't drive it all the time. He tended to save it for when he and the family went places together. The sporty two-door sedan was built like a tank and tough as nails. She sat low and hugged the corners like a champ. Plenty of power under the hood, too. Kendall enjoyed practicing the driving skills gained while in the military any chance he got.

He patted the roof of the car as he shut the door.

"Good girl," he said under his breath.

Krystal was busying herself with freeing Matthew from the car seat before settling him into the all-terrain stroller. She purchased it months ago for taking Matthew with her. Once Kendall retrieved the cooler full of snacks and grabbed the bag with their towels and toys, he closed the trunk lid and locked the car. A trio of 13.1 stickers were displayed next to a Break Neck Cross Fit Gym sticker.

The three of them headed across Pacific Ave. then Atlantic Ave., Kendall bringing up the rear. They walked across the boardwalk and made their way down to the beach.

The sun was low in the sky and the beach was empty except for a handful of people here and there. Tan sand was warm but not hot on his feet as he took his socks and shoes off. Kendall watched the waves break and tumble. They churned up sand and pieces of shells before flattening out and making a run up the sloping shore until their momentum slowed and stopped. It was as if the dry land stood at the edge of the wave's reach and declared, "no further." Only then did the water slide back from whence it came.

Kendall looked beyond the breakers, watching gentle swells rise and turn into waves then followed them until they crashed into the shore. As the water receded, he shifted his gaze back out to sea to pick another swell to focus on, observing the tides repeat their never-ending cycle over and over.

Not the big waves of your counterpart, he thought, *but you're fun to boogie board on or body surf.*

At some point, Krystal would watch Matthew by herself so he could get out there for a little while. She had promised him.

Krystal laid back in her lounge chair and relaxed for a time, eyes closed behind dark sunglasses, earbuds in playing her favorite tunes as she enjoyed the sun. Her chocolate skin glistened with sweat already. She loved this time of year.

Warm enough to be pleasant but not so hot and humid you felt like staying inside.

Most of the time, she corrected herself. *It is Virginia Beach. Damn weather here is bi-polar half the time. Never know for sure what it will be from one hour to the next.*

When they left California for Kendall to be stationed here, it took her some time to get a feel for the climate and the people. Both were different than what she had been used to. The people, in particular, were less ... tolerant. Some things carried more social stigma here than out west. She noticed how some people looked at her and Kendall back then and, even more so, how some now looked at her son. But regardless of some social hiccups, his SEAL family had welcomed them with open arms.

Krystal's brain wandered into a quiet place, the droning of the waves lulling her to sleep. After a while, she sat up and looked around. A swarm of people had arrived while she drifted off.

Meditating on the purpose of eyelids, she thought. This was her standard response to Kendall when he found her napping the last year or so.

The struggle to regain her energy and drive after giving birth was more challenging than Krystal ever thought it would be. Regardless, she had persisted, running her first half marathon since discovering she was pregnant with Matthew a mere month ago.

Krystal glanced around and noticed an unfinished sand castle. It appeared Kendall and Matthew had worked on it for some time before heading down to the water. Toy tools and buckets lay about the beginning structures that would form their fortress. She looked toward the ocean but couldn't make out any faces. Lifting the shades so she could see better, Krystal scanned the water for Kendall and Matthew amongst the throng of tourists crowding the beach now.

That's a lot of people in a short amount of time, she thought.

Glancing down at her watch, Krystal was quite surprised to see it was almost ten o'clock.

Damn, I really did conk out, didn't I? she thought.

After several seconds, she spotted them. Kendall was holding Matthew by his hands, the boy's arms stretched above his head, bright blue water wings wrapped around his biceps. The color stood in sharp contrast to his light mocha skin tone. Kendall dangled their son above the water one moment then lowered his feet into the water a few seconds later. Matthew's body sunk until his toes touched the ocean floor and Kendall lifted him back up and began the process again.

Matthew giggled like mad each time his feet touched the water.

Krystal reached into her bag and pulled out her camera. She took numerous pictures of the two of them, tracking their process as Kendall moved further out, picking Matthew up to hold him tight as he maneuvered beyond the breaking point of the waves to where the water grew calm. There he swished Matthew about in the deeper water, guiding him along in circular paths and straight lines back and forth and side to side.

Krystal reviewed the photos she had taken on the tiny built-in screen. She was a fine photographer. No wonder she made a living doing it for the last few years. Weddings, parties, family portraits, school photos, and even some glamor style shoots for military wives looking to surprise their husbands with something sexy and nice. She had a good eye.

Her eye also noted the distinct contrast of Matthew's skin tone compared to that of Kendall's paper white skin. Except for his arms, of course. He had a serious farmers tan, though farming had nothing to do with it.

She also observed Matthew's jet black, curly hair, next to Kendall's dark red beard and ginger hair.

A glorious beard, it is too, she thought, admiring her husband's appearance. *Perfect proportions and soft as silk almost.*

Krystal stood and joined her family in the water. When Matthew was ready to come ashore again, they made their way back in. Matthew toddled along ahead of them once he spotted his sand castle work in progress. Kendall helped him scoop out the moat and fetch buckets of seawater to fill it. Once finished, they both pretended sharks and crocodiles lived in the moat to eat up anyone who dared attempt to cross the final border defending their kingdom within.

Matthew grew tired after an hour of hard work. Kendall set up the large umbrella and put down a towel next to Krystal's chair for the boy to lay on and take a nap. Krystal gave Kendall a kiss then a swat on the butt.

"Go have fun," she commanded, looking toward the ocean.

Kendall grabbed the boogie board, stood at attention with it held under his left arm while he saluted with his right hand.

"Ma'am! Yes, ma'am!" he barked in play, then pivoted and took off at a slow run for the water.

Krystal took more pictures of Kendall while Matthew slept like a rock next to her. She managed to catch one of him getting rolled by a particularly large wave. She couldn't wait to show it to him. By the time Kendall exited the water, it was afternoon.

"You looked like you were having fun out there," Krystal remarked.

"Yeah," Kendall breathed a little heavy, "I did. Decent waves today but not too rough."

"I don't know, man," Krystal smiled big and shook her camera at him.

Kendall's face went slack and he stared at her.

"You got a picture of me getting rolled up by that one rogue wave, didn't you?" he demanded in jest.

"You bet your ass I did," Krystal exclaimed and laughed out loud. "You wanna see it?"

She grinned big. Kendall insisted she pull it up and they laughed together at his misfortune, now enshrined in digital color at 15 megapixels forevermore.

Kendall glanced over to confirm that Matthew was still asleep then turned back to Krystal.

"You want to do a little training?" he asked her.

Krystal cocked an eyebrow, lips pressing together and twisting to one side for a moment.

"What kind of training?" she inquired with suspicion.

"Blade tactics," Kendall said, matter of fact.

Krystal's eyes squinted together in objection.

"But we can do the movements empty handed so it doesn't draw too much attention," Kendall added without missing a beat.

Krystal looked at him for several seconds in silence, lips twitching one way then another, head tilted down. But in the end, she said "Ok."

They both stood and walked several paces away from Matthew.

"Alright, do you remember the two most important maxims when it comes to combat using a blade?" Kendall quizzed Krystal.

"Of course, I do," Krystal said and gave a frustrated sigh. "You've drilled it into me God knows how many times now." She paused, staring at him. Kendall kept his mouth shut.

"Ok," Krystal began. "One, 'Deception is the highest form of warfare' by Sun Tzu in his book The Art of War. Deception makes it easier for us to launch a preemptive strike, makes the opponent think we will be one place while we move to another."

"And, number two?" Kendall asked, not giving her a chance to continue uninterrupted. Krystal glared at him, eyes squinting and head lowering as it crept forward.

Is that a growl I hear coming from her, he thought. *Maybe it's time for me to shut up.*

"Two…" Krystal said and paused, daring Kendall to interrupt her again before continuing. "'Always attempt to stab your opponent in the face,' by Miyamoto Musashi in his work The Book of Five Rings. By attacking the eyes with empty hand or blade we make our opponent flinch. When he flinches, we have him, because he has left something else important unprotected."

Kendall nodded in approval.

"Good," he said. "So, let's just do a little random free flow. You pretend you have the blade and try to cut me."

Krystal nodded in agreement then launched her first attack. She flickered her hand out toward Kendall's eyes then, just as he committed his arm to block, she changed directions, dropping her hand down and bringing her fingers across his groin.

"Ooooh," Kendall exclaimed. "Dick cut out of the gate! It's gonna be like that huh?"

Krystal smiled big as she started to circle to her right.

"You sneaky little wench," Kendall said aloud.

Krystal laughed and then lunged in, left hand leading with a finger jab to Kendall's eyes while her pretend blade hand drove straight for his bellybutton.

She landed again.

"Dammit!" Kendall blurted out. "Maybe I shouldn't have helped you become so dangerous, huh?" They smiled at each other and laughed.

Krystal swung her hand in a forehand strike toward Kendall's neck. He slipped back, just out of range and let it go by. As Krystal reversed course and launched a backhand swing, Kendall lunged in, blocking and wrapping her arm. He hung onto her long enough to drop weight and drag her to the sand, face down. Before she could start to counter

Kendall had put both his knees on her arm, immobilizing it and pinning her body to the ground.

Krystal turned her head towards him and spit out sand.

"Oh! You *suck* mister!" Krystal declared. "I am *so* getting you back for that one!"

Kendall got up quick.

"Oh shit!" he yelped. "I'm so sorry baby. I didn't think I put you down far enough to get sand in your face."

Krystal glared at him with one baleful eye as she rubbed sand out of the other one.

"You gorilla boy. Never know your own strength. I swear."

Kendall hung his head in proverbial shame.

Right then they both heard a light cry. Their play had roused Matthew from his nap. Once awakened too soon, his temperament often took a significant dip.

"You all right, buddy?" Krystal asked as she went to Matthew and stroked his hair.

He shook his head, face screwing up in pain and fear, hand rubbing his chest.

"Oh shit," Krystal said under her breath as she noticed Matthew was breathing faster and working hard to do so, nostrils flaring, abdomen rising in an exaggerated fashion.

"Kendall…" Krystal tried not to sound concerned but her tone rose like an air raid siren as she called her husband's name.

"What is it?" Kendall asked, turning to face her while shoving their stuff into the appropriate bags and the cooler. He saw Matthew and knew at once what the problem was.

"He's having an asthma attack again, isn't he?" Kendall confirmed.

"Yes," Krystal answered, picking him up and handing him to daddy. "Hold him, rub his chest and talk to him while I find the nebulizer mask and Ventolin."

"Hey buddy boy," Kendall cooed in a higher pitch than normal. "Daddy's here, and momma's gonna get your medicine. It's gonna be ok. All right? Relax. Breathe slow. In … out … In … out."

Kendall began breathing in and out at the pace he wanted Matthew to breathe at. It seemed to be helping a little. Not a full fix but it took the edge off of it and calmed the boy down some.

"Fuck," Kendall heard Krystal say in a sharp whisper.

"What is it, Krys?" Kendall asked in a calm tone.

Krystal turned around to look at him with tears in her eyes.

"I left his medicine in the car."

"Fuck." Kendall mouthed. "Okay. It's gonna be okay. He's improved a little. Let's hurry up and go. If it holds out until we get to the car, all will be fine."

"Okay. Leave our stuff here," Krystal made the call. "You carry him and keep him calm. I'm gonna run ahead."

"No," Kendall countered her call, something he didn't do very often. "If either of us takes off right now, he'll get upset. We move together. Steady as she goes and keep the seas calm. Okay?"

Krystal wanted to argue, but she knew he was right.

"Okay," she relented and took Matthew from Kendall, so he could grab their stuff.

It was 2 pm when they left the beach, headed back to the parking lot, feet moving at steady, calm pace while Krystal's thoughts rushed ahead at breakneck speed.

*****

"Fucking hell," were the first words that sprung from Kendall's lips as he stopped in his tracks a whole three blocks away from their destination. He stood stock still, staring ahead.

"Baby," he called out to Krystal, his voice unsure and concerned. "Hold up. This is not good."

Krystal hadn't looked far enough ahead yet to see the huge crowd occupying most of the public parking lot where their car was. Kendall moved in front of his wife, scanning right and left, assessing every detail for any information that would give him insight into what the hell was going on.

"Stay behind me," he said in a flat tone, waving her to follow as he moved out at a slow walk.

Kendall noticed one side of the parking lot was full of a couple of hundred people, both men and women, dressed in black. Many were of dark skin tone, either African American or Hispanic, but there were plenty of white people mixed in with them as well. Some of them held signs. Others stood on the back of vehicles lifting a banner in the air.

He couldn't make out the words on the banner at this distance, but he saw one sign displaying a Nazi swastika and the 'buster' circle with a line through it. Right then someone hoisted a large red flag with a black circle in the middle and a red flag overlaying a black flag. Kendall recognized it.

"Oh shit," Kendall muttered. "It's an Antifa rally… how the fuck?" His words trailed off in disbelief as he continued studying the crowd.

The middle ground was filled with law enforcement, many with riot shields and gear. Behind them were several cops on horseback moving back and forth along the line of officers. Beyond them was another line of riot police facing the opposite direction, toward a crowd of all white people.

This other group was mostly men with shaved heads, though there were some women present amongst them as well. Their standard dress seemed to be blue jeans with T-shirts bearing swastikas, confederate flags or various Germanic and Celtic symbols that identified their white European ancestry. Some were, no doubt, bikers, also. Their leather jackets with various identifying patches gave it away.

They had their own variety of signs. Kendall spotted one with a white-hooded man, his fist in the air, and a second one, the background black and the word PRIDE in large white letters.

"Oh, for fuck's sake!" he exclaimed. "The white supremacists are here too? What in the hell is going on?"

Kendall was at a loss.

"Krystal, how did I miss that some big rally was taking place down here on Memorial Day? How *in the hell* did I miss that announcement?"

Krystal had been quiet up until this point, just taking everything in, but now she spoke.

"Kendall, aren't we parked right in the middle of that mess? Like, not far from where the police are standing in between them?"

Kendall looked closer.

"Fuck me! You're right," he admitted.

"Well, how the hell are we going to get to our car?" she asked him.

"Give me a second," he said, frustration with the situation and with himself for not having been aware this was going on today, edging his voice.

He stopped and stared ahead. Krystal could almost see the cogs turning in his head a hundred miles per hour. After several seconds he blurted out his plan.

"You and Matthew stay here. I'll go get the car and pick you up. If I get hurt, you call the police and EMS and go back to the Boardwalk and wait for them to come to you."

Kendall turned around and looked Krystal in the eye.

"Y'all stay the fuck away from those lunatics," he ordered, assuming command.

Krystal was used to that being his initial response in dangerous circumstances. But he was used to her not obeying if she disagreed.

"I don't think so," Krystal informed him, blunt as a hammer.

"If you go in there by yourself," she argued, "either side may get pissed off with you for not supporting their agenda. I have no doubt that one group or the other would pick a fight with you and end up swarming you. We've seen it in videos of other gatherings. Just because someone doesn't support them they get pissy and then they get violent. But…" and she paused for emphasis and shifted Matthew to her opposite hip, "if we all go, we're probably guaranteed to at least get treated decently by the social justice crowd. I mean, we're a goddamned biracial couple with a little biracial kid, right? The white supremacists will hate us, but if we can approach more from the Antifa side, we should be good."

Kendall shook his head as they held each other's gaze.

"I don't like this, Krystal," he said, gritting his teeth.

"I don't care," she responded with a blunt finality he knew all too well. "I'm not sending you in there by yourself to get hurt when I think my idea will get us all out of this unscathed."

"But," Kendall started to say. Krystal cut him off.

"No 'but'," she stated with firm resolve, "I'm going with you. You ready or what?"

She gave Kendall the head wag and opened her eyes wide, eyebrows lifting high on her forehead as she stood her ground. Her face all but said, "Fight me, I dare you."

Kendall knew better.

"All right," he conceded. "You've got your knife on you, though, right?" he asked.

Krystal lifted her shirt to show the small fixed blade clipped to the inside of her shorts waistband.

"Ok, then," Kendall said. "Let's go. But we leave the baby carriage here. We can get it afterward."

Without another word, he turned to face the crowd of protesters.

As they drew nearer Krystal could read several of the signs the Antifa protesters were lifting up and down. Some of them chanted the slogan on display as well.

"**MAKE RACISTS AFRAID AGAIN**"

"**ALL MY HEROES KILL COPS**"

"**GOOD NIGHT ALT RIGHT**" This one had a picture of a white guy wearing a Nazi swastika shirt getting punched in the face.

"**NAZIS NOT WELCOME HERE**"

"**W.W.C.A.D. – WHAT WOULD CAPTAIN AMERICA DO?**"

"**WE PUNCH NAZIS**"

"**SMASH THE STATE. AMERICA WAS NEVER GREAT.**" This one made Krystal's hackles rise on edge. To her, it was a direct assault on her husband's service in the military, fighting for their country and way of life.

Though she could agree with some of their principal beliefs, like punching Nazis, Krystal could not condone their violent methods and often anti-white sentiments. Racism was racism to her, no matter the skin color.

Across the police border, Krystal could read the white supremacist's protest signs as well.

"WHITE RIGHTS. WHITE EQUALITY. WHITE FREEDOM."

"WHITE POWER"

"WHITES WILL RULE AGAIN"

"PROUD MY ANCESTORS WERE COLONIALISTS"

"THE NEW BARBARIANS"

"WHITES ARE JUST BETTER AT CONQUERING PEOPLE"

"NO GUILT HERE. WE LOVE OUR RACE."

"JOIN THE RESISTANCE."

"FUCK THE POLICE"

Geez, thought Krystal. *A bunch of vapid, simpletons who can't see past their small corner of the world. If ignorance is a disease, then they're all terminally infected.*

*****

Roy MacCreedy stood toe to toe with the man before him, who, though large in his own right, was much smaller than Roy, and nowhere near as muscular.

Roy looked down his nose at this other man, Henry Tate. Henry was wearing a dress uniform with khaki pants and button-up shirt, sporting various patches, including a swastika, one with Hitler giving a Sieg heil, and two others with acronyms – ANA for the Aryan National Alliance and WNM for White Nationalist Movement. His hair was cropped short as well as his beard. Beside him was a man dressed in khaki slacks, burgundy dress shoes, and a light blue polo shirt with the letters NPI – National Policy Institute embroidered on the pocket.

He remained silent the entire time.

Roy, by comparison, was wearing faded blue jeans, some big black leather boots, a white muscle shirt and a sleeveless denim jacket with a big swastika patch on the back as well as the letters AB embroidered for Aryan Brotherhood. His head was shaved bald, but his red beard was full and rather long. Tattoos covered his arms. Werewolf SS soldiers crashing through a door inspired by the movie American Werewolf in London covered his right arm while a swastika, SS lightning bolts, a noose, a burning cross and the white power fist all decorated his left arm.

Behind Roy stood two young men, both rather lanky. Richie had a backpack thrown over his shoulder, but Lenny carried nothing. They kept their mouths shut because both of them knew better than to talk for Roy. If he wanted Richie and Lenny to say something, he'd tell them to say it.

"What did you say to me and my boys?" Roy repeated himself as he took a step closer to the man. Henry Tate gulped big, then asserted himself despite the fear he was feeling.

"I said," he managed, "we don't want you here. You guys are not representing the cause. Hell, your brothers will team up with fucking spics and kikes if it suits their agenda and will make them money. Y'all are sell outs. That's why we don't want you here. So, leave, why don't ya? Just leave." Henry Tate finished saying his piece, feeling a weight lifted off his chest now that he had done the deed. But he didn't want to hang around for any potential fallout, so Henry turned to walk away.

Roy grabbed his shoulder and spun him back around.

"Look fuck face, I'm done with listening to y'all go soft. You limp-spined fuckers can't even bring yourself to call someone a nigger in public. You disgust me almost as much as all those parasitic races fucking white men out of their jobs and taking their women.

Roy was livid.

"So, fuck you, Henry!" Roy shouted, pointing a thick finger in Henry's face. "Fuck you and your dickless buddy here!" Roy nodded at the NPI man in the light blue polo. "My people aren't going anywhere! You and yours are the problem! Y'all got soft! Don't want to knock heads! Scared to fight the police and go to jail! You're the traitors to the cause! Not the Brotherhood! We're here today to show you what real white power looks like. Now," Roy took another step forward, bringing his nose within inches of the other man's forehead, "get *the fuck* out of my face you yellow back losers."

Roy stared at Henry. Henry wanted to square up but knew he was out of his league and to do so would get their rally shut down. He kept his mouth closed, turned around and walked away, the NPI man following.

Roy turned to Lenny and Richie.

"Fuck them," he said, his words all blunt force. "You got the cocktails in that bag ready to go, right Richie?"

Richie nodded his head in excitement. "Yes sir, Roy!"

"Alrighty, then," Roy said. "Let's stir some shit up, then let those cocktails fly. Show everybody here that White Power is still real."

*****

As they got closer, the noise disturbed Matthew. His basic human instincts felt the threat in the air. Unlike an adult, he couldn't run, and he couldn't fight. Fear was all his mind could do.

That fear infected his body with stress. The stress pushed him back into excited breathing. Krystal did her best to comfort her son and keep him calm.

"He's getting worse again," she told Kendall. "We've got to get to his medicine ASAP."

Kendall nodded in agreement and touched his son's head before turning to move out again.

They cut down 18th street to Arctic Ave to come up on the south side of the parking lot. They approached from the Antifa side of the protest, making their way towards where the riot police stood arrayed. Entering near the front of the Antifa crowd would give them the most direct path to where their car was parked. There was a sudden uproar from the battle line. Kendall looked to see what was going on. Things had boiled over at last. Antifa and Aryan protesters were throwing stuff at each other - bottles, rocks, and anything else hard they happened to be holding. Some of them were trying to push past the police to fight with the other side.

A police officer on horseback raised a bullhorn and told everyone to disperse.

Thank God, Kendall thought. Both sides were irate, but their animosity shifted targets at that moment and they raised their fists and voices in unison against their common enemy - law enforcement.

"Let's hurry up," Kendall told Krystal, "Get to the car while they're all focused on the police."

Krystal nodded in agreement and they moved out, squeezing in between people at the perimeter then pressing through the crowd toward their car - their ticket out of this hellhole nightmare and the treasure chest holding her son's medicine. Krystal took the lead, relying on people's common courtesy toward women and children to make way for her, Kendall tucked in tight behind his wife.

They were almost to the car when someone grabbed Kendall's shoulder from behind and spun him around. Kendall turned to look at two large men. They were easily six-four and three hundred pounds each, compared to Kendall's six-two and two-hundred-pound frame. They were dressed alike and both wearing wraparound, mirrored sunglasses. Biggie Smalls twins. The only way he could tell them apart was by the bandannas they wore over their lower faces. One of them was blue and the other red.

I can't just punch these fuckers or kick their kneecaps in, he thought as he looked from one man to the other. *It'll bring everybody nearby down on me. I've got to play it cool. Maybe Krystal can at least make it to the car.*

"Is there a problem fellas?" Kendall asked in a loud voice above the noise of the crowd.

"Where do you think you're going?" Biggie Smalls blue asked, his brow knitted into a knot between his squinted eyes.

"You have to help us fight the cops and those fucking Nazis," Biggie Smalls red commanded. "All in, or not in at all."

Motherfucker went through Kendall's brain but more productive words made it out of his mouth.

"Umm… guys, no offense, but I'm afraid there's a misunderstanding. My wife and I are just trying to get to our car. Our son is…"

"Trying to cut out on us when the shit gets real, huh?" Red cut him off.

"No," Kendall stated, feeling frustrated and starting to look pissed. "I was never with y'all. I parked my car here this morning and went to the fucking beach. My wife and I are just trying to get our son *back* to the car and get his medicine."

"Never with us?" Red exclaimed, his voice booming, his face shaking beneath the bandana as he spit the words out. "You with those Nazis, motherfucker?" The man pushed Kendall. Hard.

Kendall exercised self-control, restraining the desire in every fiber of his body to punch Red in the throat. He raised his hands, palms out in front of him in a non-aggressive show of compliance.

"Fuck no, guys!" he shouted emphatically. "I'm not with those fucking racists. I'm not with anybody."

Krystal looked back and realized Kendall wasn't with her anymore. She began scanning the crowd looking for him.

Goddammit. He's got the keys.

She began walking back the way she came. It only took a few seconds for her to spot Kendall trying to de-escalate things with two big guys. She could hear one of the men yell at her husband.

"If you ain't one of us, *you're one of them*!!"

Biggy Smalls blue stepped up and tried to push Kendall. Kendall deflected the man's hands away, though, stepping to the side and turning into him. Kendall stepped into Blue then, pushing him on an angle by his shoulder and upper arm. The man stumbled a few feet. Red stepped up, drawing back to punch.

Krystal lunged in front of Kendall trying to diffuse the situation.

"STOP!" she yelled. "He's my husband!"

Red didn't care. He punched Krystal in the face, dropping her flat, then drew back to punch Kendall too.

Rage overcame Kendall in the amount of time it took for the Red's hand to retract after striking Krystal.

He exploded forward, launching a front kick into the man's kneecap, hyper-extending it and causing Red's upper body to bow forward beyond his knee, forcing him off balance. Kendall clubbed Red's neck with his left arm then cupped the back of the man's head. His right hand rose up, chopping Red in the throat then clamped down around his larynx, squeezing tight. Red's body dropped to get away from the pain, sitting him down on his ass. Kendall folded Red's head down as he released his hold on the throat and raised his right arm high in the air. Kendall relaxed his legs, letting his whole weight fall, feet stomping the ground as he brought the bone of his forearm down on the base of the Red's skull.

Lights out. The man collapsed into an unconscious heap. Biggie Smalls blue, who was coming back for more, stopped dead in his tracks.

Kendall spit on the downed man's face and turned around to help Krystal up. She had held onto enough consciousness to keep a grip on Matthew and remain in a seated position.

"C'mon baby," she heard Kendall say, felt his arms wrap under her and lift, felt her weight settle on her feet once more. "Just hold on tight to Matthew," he encouraged. The wobble in her legs still present, Kendall helped Krystal walk, one foot in front of the other, shoving his way through people without giving a damn who might not like it.

A roar went up from both sides of the crowd. Batons cracked against riot shields in warning. The mounted officers formed two lines, one facing each side of the protest. Turning their horses sideways to form a wall they began moving forward. People began screaming. Many scrambled to retreat.

Kendall heard a horse cry out in pain followed by a man shrieking at the top of his lungs.

Kendall turned around to see a horse and its rider ablaze, the flames engulfing one of the riot police standing next to them, as well. Kendall watched another Molotov cocktail fly through the air and crash next to the burning horse, spraying its contents onto the lower body of another officer. The horse tried to throw his rider and take off, but the officer ended up tangled in the saddle stirrups. His body hung down, but he managed to hold onto the reins, preventing his head from bouncing off the pavement as the animal trampled several of the riot police in a straight line. The horse was burning bright, running in a blind panic, trying to escape the very flames it was fanning into greater hunger.

The wall of horses broke into disarray as the riders struggled to prevent their steeds from panicking at the sight of the flames. Moments later, Kendall saw a red mist burst into the air at several points along the police line. It only took a second for him to smell it and realize what was happening.

Pepper spray.

He spotted the economy size, crowd control foggers in the hands of a few of the mounted police officers now. They were saturating both sides of the crowd with the aerosol in hopes of scattering them and restoring control.

"Shit!" Kendall shouted. "They're hosing down everyone with pepper spray, Krystal! Hurry up! We have to get in the car NOW!!!"

Matthew's already coughing and wheezing in between crying at the top of his shitty lungs, Kendall thought. *That shit could kill him in his current state.*

Krystal understood the implications the instant she heard the words 'pepper spray' and forced her legs to move faster even as she buried Matthew's face in her chest. The car was in sight. Just another ten feet.

They split up, Krystal holding herself up on the hood of the car as she made her way to the passenger door even as Kendall rushed to put the key in the driver door.

"HEY!" Kendall heard a man's voice shout. "That guy and his bitch killed Jerry! GET THEM!!!"

I didn't kill that fucker, Kendall thought, scrambling to open the door and unlock the car. *It won't matter, anyway. Perception is king right now.*

As he jumped into the driver's seat and started it up, Krystal got in, shut her door and hit the lock button. He looked up and saw numerous people turn and stare at them, murder in their eyes. They rushed the car, baseball bats and flagpoles smashing down on the hood of the vehicle. The passenger window exploded inward, pieces of glass covering Krystal and Matthew as she hunted for his medicine in the console.

"Aaaahhh" Krystal screamed, face flinching away from the glass, body shielding Matthew.

A man reached inside, brass knuckles on one hand, and grabbed Krystal's right upper arm. She tried to jerk away but the man's grip was unmoving. Rank sweat filled her nostrils as he tried to force his upper body inside to get both hands on her.

At that same moment a baseball bat blew out Kendall's window, He turned away, protecting his eyes but looked back an instant later, just in time to see the knife thrusting at his neck. Kendall managed to raise his elbow up and deflect the man's hand, the point of the knife ripping a gouge in Kendall's scalp as it cleared the top of his head. Kendall caught the man's hand and wrapped his other arm around the man's elbow from underneath. Pulling it into his body, he secured the arm long enough to throw the car in drive and punch the gas.

The man squalled in stunned surprise.

Mr. Brass knuckles, holding onto Krystal, got off easy, the passenger door frame knocking his hands loose and leaving him behind. The other guy wasn't so lucky. Kendall held on, first causing the man's elbow to hyper-extend against the B pillar and then dragging him for about twenty yards, wailing in Kendall's left ear the whole time, as he plowed down several other protesters who were coming for their vehicle with weapons.

Kendall stayed in the gas, knocking people off to each side while a couple of them tumbled over the hood, windshield, and roof. Despite the chaos, the smashing of bones and the deep, dull thud of his car impacting against bodies was clearly audible to him. A bloody skull imprint left the front windshield broken, the spiderweb cracks reaching for the edges. A bit of flesh and hair remained behind at the center of the crater.

Once the man with the knife was no longer standing, Kendall let go of the guy's arm. The car bucked as part of him tumbled under the rear tire. There was a crunching noise and another scream. Two hands on the wheel, now, Kendall looked for a way out of the parking lot but was blocked by the horses. He slammed on the brakes.

"Shit!" Krystal yelled, bracing out on the glovebox with one hand. She looked at the glovebox with sudden hope.

Is that where I put his medicine? she thought.

She pulled the handle and it opened, revealing Matthew's medicine on top of the vehicle registration, in plain sight. She put the medicine in the hand holding Matthew and secured him to her body. It would protect him from being banged into anything and help prevent him from breathing in any pepper spray.

One of the horses shifted to the right, leaving a gap. Kendall punched the gas and shot through it only to plunge into the midst of the white supremacists. Several of them dove out of the way but he clipped a few of them as well. Kendall saw a closed metal gate and hit the brakes.

Blocked, Kendall thought and started scanning for an opening.

Chaos ruled.

People ran everywhere, some hacking and coughing, some fighting other protesters, some attacking the police, bringing several down. He heard a new man's voice shouting.

"That white son of a bitch just tried to kill us!"

Kendall looked in his mirror. The man pointing a finger at them was a huge, Viking looking beast of a man. Musclebound, bald head, long beard, and at least six-five.

"He's got a black girlfriend and a mother-fuckin' chocolate swirl kid, too! KILL 'EM!!"

The man ripped off his shirt then threw back his head like a wolf and howled.

Fuck me, Kendal thought. *As if the Antifa guys weren't bad enough. That dude just wants to see the world burn and we're next on the menu.*

Not everyone responded to the man's command. Kendall noticed there were three distinctly different modes of dress amongst these white supremacist protesters – uniform khaki pants with tan button-up shirts and patches, white-collar men with casual dress and then the biker types with jeans, cut off shirts, tattoos, boots and leather jackets. The men and women dressed like bikers were the ones who obeyed the mountain of a man, turning to rush toward Kendall and Krystal's vehicle, faces full of hate.

"Hold on!" Kendall warned Krystal as he snapped the wheel and pumped the e-brake to kick out the ass end then pumped it again to release it. He slammed the gas down, pushing the rear end all the way around 180 degrees, slapping four men with the rear quarter panel and tire. They flew through the air, a good ten feet. Two of them slammed into a van, bones fracturing, then tumbled to the pavement, groaning. The other two missed the van but beaned the light post, one head first, neck collapsing down like a turtle retreating into its shell, the other sideways, his lower back folding backward on impact, one of his kidneys rupturing from the brutal force.

Krystal's body bashed her door from the sudden weight transfer. It almost knocked the wind out of her, but she managed to hold on tight to Matthew, still. She looked down at him. He was struggling to breathe, unable to make a single noise when any normal child his age or older would be bawling their head off. His lips were turning a bluish hue. Krystal gripped the oh shit handle at the top edge of her window and held on tight to stabilize herself for any more radical weight transfers like the Bootleg turn Kendall had just performed.

No sooner did she secure herself than Kendall snapped the wheel to the right, throwing the weight and tapping the brake at the same time to make the ass end kick out and the front to rotate 90 degrees. He hit the gas again and took off for what he thought was an opening. As people moved out of the way, though, Kendall realized too late there was a car on the other side of them, sitting broadside.

It's rammable, he thought without hesitation, and lined his car up to hit the rear tire of the vehicle. He floored the gas pedal and stayed in it all the way through impact. The ass end of the parked vehicle swung out like a door on hinges.

Oh shit was all he had time to think before he hit the second, but smaller car, that was hiding one sparking space over, knocking it into a pickup truck sitting right next to it.

Instant stop.

Krystal barely hung onto Matthew and the oh shit handle as they struck the second vehicle, and everything slammed to a halt.

"Fuck!!!" Kendall yelled. Looking ahead, though, he could see that on the other side of the pick-up truck, on Krystal's side, was a bush hedge with a gap in it and then the street.

"Get out!" Kendall hollered at Krystal.

"What?" She cried in confusion.

"I said get the fuck out! Run!" He pointed with his finger in front of her face to the space in between the bushes. "There's your way out! Get Matthew out of here. I'll hold 'em off!"

"No!" Krystal shouted in disbelief.

"*NOW*!!" Kendall roared, neck muscles distended.

She had never heard him sound that way. In the back of her brain, she knew he was right. It's the kind of thing they had trained together. As much as she hated the thought of leaving Kendall, she had to obey him this time. She popped the door open, Matthew held to her body with medicine in hand.

Krystal shut the door behind her and yelled out "I love you!" as she took off, not sparing the time to even look back.

She had to get away. Get to a safe place and give Matthew his medicine. It could be too late already. The pepper spray had been tickling her lungs for the last couple of minutes, a cough crouching at the back of her throat. It might have already compromised Matthew beyond the ability of the medicine to help him recover if he breathed too much of the pepper spray in.

Kendall slapped the car in reverse and turned around to look over his shoulder, hand at twelve o'clock on the wheel as he stomped the gas pedal and peeled out, steering the vehicle directly at the people moving his way. As his car bore down on the group of attackers, they parted like the Red Sea, jumping off to either side. Kendall timed his turn around, snapping the wheel from twelve to six o'clock, causing the front end to swing around a full 180 degrees, smacking two men before slamming it into drive and taking off again. They cartwheeled over the hood of his car before crashing head first into the pavement. Their necks folded at unnatural angles, legs jerking in a spastic fashion, as if from a jolt of electricity.

It's working, he thought to himself, elated that Krystal and Matthew were going to get away. *They're completely focused on me right now.*

Kendall eyed an additional small group of potential attackers and launched into another Bootleg. Most of them dove out of the way, but one of them was behind the curve. The rear end caught his legs, flipping him upside down into the air, where he hung for a second before plummeting back to the earth, face hitting first, feet folding over his hips until they slapped the back of his own head.

Kendall howled in victory and hammered the wheel with one hand.

A moment later the world caught fire. A Molotov cocktail someone tossed through his broken driver's window ignited his whole body.

He tried to scream but the flames were licking up the oxygen. He slammed on the brakes, opened the door, and dove out, covering his face with his hands as he hit the ground to stop, drop and roll in a desperate attempt to put the blaze out.

The world spun out of control for Kendall, his body tumbling over and over, extinguishing the fire but only after gross damage was inflicted. His nerve fibers screamed in agony.

Without warning, his body came to a sudden stop. He felt the pressure of someone's boot on his back. He moved his hands away from his face. Part of his cheeks and forehead were stuck to his palms. Gloved hands grabbed his wrists and pulled him forward then pinned his face to the concrete curb.

A voice made its way into his ear canal.

"You Kunta Kinte fucking son of a bitch. I'm gonna kill that little abomination you call your kid, then I'm gonna fuck your nigger whore and kill her too. I just wanted you to know you *won't* be around to stop me."

Kendall felt a flash of intense pain as the mammoth Viking leader curb-stomped the back of his head.

The world went black and Kendall never woke up again. The stomps continued, knee rising high, hands in the air, before the booted foot fell again. Over and over it repeated, bones cracking, blood flowing, gray matter seeping out, before the man stopped at last, breathing heavy from his exertion.

"Fuck yeah, Roy!" one of his followers hollered. "I recorded that shit too!"

"I don't give a shit," Roy said, blunt as a hammer. "Where'd that bitch go to?"

"I saw where she took off to, Roy," the tall, skinny man wearing a white muscle shirt said, excited to please his boss.

"Good, Lenny," Roy praised him. "Now, grab Richie and start after her. I'll follow but don't wait for me. You two are my fastest boys. Catch that colored bitch!"

"You got it, boss!" Lenny assured Roy, then turned around, scanning for Richie. He spotted him right off running away from the police line where he had just thrown another Molotov cocktail.

Lenny yelled, waving his arms above his head as he did so.

"Richie! Hey, Richie!" Richie looked around and saw Lenny.

"Get yer ass over here!" Lenny directed, waving him to hurry up with both hands. "Pronto!"

*****

Krystal heard the howl from that beast of a man again. She tried not to cry and jogged on, cradling Matthew with one arm as she rubbed his chest and tried to calm him down.

She looked back and saw black roiling pillars of smoke rising up into the sky. She knew what the man's howl of triumph likely meant.

Kendall's dead. The thought burned through her brain and straight to her heart. Tears welled up in her eyes and it was difficult to talk to Matthew.

"It's gonna be ok, Matthew, baby. Daddy made sure we're safe."

Matthew panted for oxygen, wheezing and coughing in between every couple of shallow breaths before trying to cry. Unable to do so, the cycle started again.

Krystal ducked behind a parked vehicle and squatted down, leaning back on the sedan's passenger door for support as she scrambled to load the Ventolin into the nebulizer mask.

"Lady. Help me." The weak voice was like gravel sliding over glass.

Krystal startled, almost dropping the mask as her head snapped right. One car down, leaned upright against another vehicle, was a police officer. His face was bloody and burnt along with his arms.

"Oh my god," Krystal whispered. "What happened to you?"

"Molotov … cocktail," the man managed to groan. "My horse bolted … eventually, I fell off … dropped and rolled."

He coughed and spit blood up into his lap. Crimson stained phlegm hung from his mouth along with a white froth.

"Please. Help me. Call 911. Tell them … I'm here."

"Don't you have a radio?" Krystal asked without thinking.

"Melted," the officer said and glanced down at the disfigured mic on his lapel. Krystal looked down at his hip. The radio looked the same.

Krystal glanced back up at the man, meeting his eyes, then went back to taking care of the medicine for her son.

"I'm sorry," she said, not looking at him as she spoke. "My son is having an asthma attack. I have to help him."

"Call 911. Get them coming for your son and me. It's your best chance. And mine."

Krystal considered his words.

He's right, she thought. *I might not be able to fix this if it's too far gone. I need EMS to be on the way.*

She pulled out her phone and punched in the numbers 911.

"What's your name?" she asked the officer.

"Thomas … Santiago …"

It rang three times before the dispatcher picked up.

"Virginia Beach Police Department. What is your emergency?"

When she opened her mouth to speak, Krystal's emotions overflowed but she managed to keep her words concise even if excited.

"Hello! My name is Krystal Pittman. I'm at the corner of 22nd Street and Baltic Avenue. My 13-month-old son is having a severe asthma attack. Officer Thomas Santiago is also here and he is hurt badly. Burned and having trouble breathing. We were both attacked by the protesters. We need EMS and Police. Now! Please!"

"I understand. Dispatching EMS and Police officers to your location now. Please stay on the line."

Krystal put the phone on speaker mode and began preparing the mask to place over Matthew's face and administer the medicine that would help unlock the boy's restricted little airways. It was then she heard the hoots and hollers no more than a couple blocks away and a voice yelling "That bitch went this way, Roy! I saw her!"

Fear shot through Krystal's heart like an arrow piercing the liver of some poor animal. Her head spun, and she looked at the officer. She tried to say she was sorry with her eyes as she stared at him. She rocked forward and raised herself into a low squat and moved away from the voices until she could scurry, bent over, to the other side of the street and slip behind another vehicle, kneeling next to a pickup truck's front tire.

Krystal began scanning her surroundings for a way out or a better place to hide.

"Woooo!!!" she heard a victorious call from one of the white supremacists. "Found a wounded pig, Roy! One of 'em Richie lit up earlier ... He's *all* fucked up," Lenny declared. It was a minute before Krystal heard Roy's voice, but when she did, she froze, not wanting to make a sound.

"Well, well, well. We've got ourselves some Barb-B-Q Pork, boys!" Roy shouted as he trotted up.

"Fuck you ... you skin-headed ... bastards" Officer Santiago managed to wheeze out.

Roy and his boys laughed at Santiago.

"Fucker thinks he's hard, don't he?" Roy asked Lenny and Richie.

"I think he does, boss," Richie said. "Kinda disrespectful if you ask me."

Roy cut a look at Richie.

"Well, I didn't ask you, you dumb sumbitch. But … I think you're right. And disrespect can't go unpunished."

Roy squatted down in front of Santiago, his face mere inches from Santiago's, glaring into the dying man's eyes.

"You think you're hard, huh, motherfucker?" Roy asked in a calm but cold tone.

"Yeah …" Santiago answered and coughed. He looked Roy dead in the eyes and refused to turn away. "C'mon Roy … punish me. I'm good for it … Try …" Another cough, this time more violent and bloody. "Try to make me scream … Take your time …"

Santiago cracked a hellish smile, the skin on his face parting as if each crack were smiling too.

Roy cocked his head sideways for a few seconds.

"This fucker is too happy for a dying man. Unless he thinks his death is going to have value…"

Roy stood up like a shot.

"The cops are on their way!" he announced. "Fuck you pig," he said, looking down at Santiago.

Krystal decided to peek around the truck's front end at the worst possible moment.

Roy took a step back, loading his power leg, then lashed out a front kick straight into Santiago's face with his size fifteen lug-soled boot. Rapid fire, again and again, he kicked the officer's face, caving it in before the man's body fell over. Once down, Roy stomped the bloody head a few more times to make sure he was dead.

"All right," Roy said, breathing a little heavy, "let's get out of here before the cops come in like the cavalry. I want to find that bitch before she slips away."

Matthew started to cough again, making wheezing sounds.

Oh God, no! Krystal's mind screamed. She shifted the nebulizer mask into the hand holding Matthew and covered her son's mouth with her free hand.

"Shhhhhhh baby … Please …" she begged Matthew, wishing he could understand the dire severity of their situation.

"Did you guys hear something?" Roy asked Lenny and Richie.

The two young men stopped everything and stood still, listening to see if they heard anything.

Krystal kept her hand over Matthew's mouth.

My God, I'm going to smother him if I don't let him breathe soon, Krystal told herself. *But if I take my hand away right now, we're both going to die … I've got to move. Now!*

Krystal scanned for some avenue of escape leading away from Roy and his men. About twenty meters ahead to her left she spotted an alleyway. She could scramble over to it still moving away from Roy and his men. She kept low and ran, stepping as lightly as she could while still covering Matthew's mouth. As soon as she hit the alley she exploded into a full sprint. Ahead were a wall and an opening to the right.

That's got to lead to another alley that connects with the next street over, she thought.

Krystal rounded the corner to face a dead end. It wasn't an alleyway at all. It was the entrance to the rear of a closed down funeral home, for the hearses to deliver the bodies for preparation out of sight.

"Oh, no," Krystal said aloud to herself and then thought, *I hope they didn't see me come in here.*

At that moment, Krystal realized Matthew wasn't coughing anymore and looked down to check, her heart thumping like a jackhammer all of a sudden.

Matthew wasn't breathing. His head and limbs hung limp.

"O, God!" Krystal shrieked in a panic and knelt down, laying Matthew on the ground. She placed the Nebulizer mask over his face then did a chin lift, head tilt maneuver to open his airway and bent down, placing her ear to his chest. There was no pitter-pat sound coming from his heart. No fog on the inside of the mask from him breathing.

"Fuck, fuck, fuck!" she said in quick succession, trying to be quiet as she pinched his cheeks with her fingers to open his mouth.

Chest compressions, she thought. *I should do chest compressions. Maybe it will help draw the medicine into his lungs as well as help restart his heart.*

She laid the other hand on his sternum in line with his nipples and began one-handed compressions.

"God!" she spat under her breath. "Please don't let me lose my baby too! Please!"

"One and two and three and four and five and six and seven …" she counted out loud to help herself focus, continuing until she reached one and thirty before stopping to assess again.

Still no fog on the inside of the mask. She pulled it off and gave Matthew two breaths then started compressions again.

"One and two and three and four and five and six and seven …" she called out loud, struggling not to begin bawling as she tried to save her son. When she reached one and thirty again she gave him two more breaths.

His chest spasmed. A violent cough escaped his lungs as he began to breathe again.

"Oh God! Thank you! Thank you!" She cried out as the tears streamed down her cheeks. She pulled the Nebulizer mask back over Matthew's face, cradled him in her arms, and sat back against the brick wall.

Her body went limp, the constant adrenaline coursing through her system for the last half hour or so ceased production and she crashed, hard, both body and emotions.

Sobs wracked Krystal's chest, causing it to heave up and down as she thought of Kendall and Matthew, one stolen from her and one barely preserved. Before she knew it, the world went black. Whether she passed out or fell asleep she could not tell.

*****

The feeling of Matthew being ripped out of her arms snatched Krystal back into a conscious state. Eyes opening wide with terror, she followed the feel of Matthew's fleeting flesh as they were separated.

Roy stood there, holding Matthew upside down, gripping his ankles together like a baseball bat handle.

"You, your husband, and your little abomination here, never should have come anywhere near us today," Roy informed Krystal with blunt indifference to her pain and cold hatred in his eyes.

Matthew began screaming. The mask did little to minimize the intensity of his cries.

"Please …" Krystal begged, the single word little more than a sigh falling out of her open mouth.

"Whaddaya say, fellas?" Roy called out. "Batter up?"

"*NO!*" Krystal shrieked. She tried to lunge to her feet. Richie kicked her in the chest, knocking her back into the wall, where she bounced off and landed on her side, gasping for air.

"Swing batter, batter, swing!" Lenny shouted, his voice reverberating off the walls.

Krystal watched, helpless, as Roy's upper body torqued to his right, flicking Matthew's body around behind him. Without a second of hesitation, he stepped toward the brick wall, snapping his arms and hips forward in one coordinated, explosive movement. It all happened in such a blur, Krystal's brain didn't even have a chance to slow her perceptions down. One moment Matthew was dangling in the air, alive, the next moment she saw his head crumple on impact with the wall, his cries cut short in an instant.

Krystal shrieked like a banshee. Before she could move, Roy drew back and swung again. Another crack resounded all about her.

"*You fucking bastard*!" she screamed. "*I'm gonna fucking kill you!*"

Krystal attempted to stand, right hand going for her blade. Roy drew back once more, and this time Matthew's skull met Krystal's forehead. Her world fell into a deep darkness rising from the depths of unconscious oblivion.

*****

How'd I end up on a boat? was Krystal's first conscious thought before realizing the rocking of her body wasn't from ocean waves. There was one sharp pain after another in between her legs, inside her, each one accompanied by the impact of flesh against her buttocks.

She felt the hand palming her skull, pinning the left side of her face to the ground. The pressure against her temples was excruciating but she sucked it up and didn't make a sound, even when the back and forth movement of her head ground her cheek against the asphalt like a cheese grater with every punishing thrust of Roy's hips.

Krystal opened her eyes a crack to look around. In the low light, she spotted her knife lying within arm's reach of her right hand.

He must have taken it out of my waistband and set it down, Krystal thought, *or it fell out when he ripped my pants off.*

Kendall's voice spoke in her head, quoting Sun Tzu's Art of War.

"Deception is the highest form of warfare."

He had taught her how to fight dirty, how to be sneaky, and how to use a knife to kill.

By God, she swore to herself, *if I can find an opening, I'm going to fuck this man up six ways to Sunday.*

The pain inside Krystal suddenly increased as Roy's size did, but she continued to play possum, doing her best not to tense up and let him know she was awake. She laid there, waiting, taking the abuse in the hope of surviving and getting revenge.

Roy slammed inside her twice more before locking out his hips and groaning, his whole body rigid when he climaxed.

She felt a warmth deep inside that made her stomach heave involuntarily in disgust. But it also gave rise to a righteous rage. This violation was the coup de grace of atrocities stacked upon atrocities, the final blow that broke something inside her and set a demon free.

Krystal stared at the knife and struggled to stay immobile while she waited for an opportunity to act. Several seconds later Roy's body relaxed. He sat back on his heels, releasing the pressure on her skull. The second she felt nothing restraining her, Krystal moved with blinding speed and absolute commitment – all or nothing.

She grabbed the knife handle in a reverse grip position, the tip of the blade pointing down. Pressing up off the ground with both hands she twisted her body to turn towards Roy, kicking out with her right foot into his upper chest as she spun in front of him, a shouting, blur of movement.

"DIE!!"

Roy was caught off guard by her ambush. Knocked backward, while still kneeling, he lost his balance. His legs folded underneath him as his hands reflexively reached down to catch himself. Krystal did not waste the opportunity she had created but continued her attack, lunging forward to swing the knife through the air with a backhand thrust to Roy's neck.

It landed.

Roy tried to bring his arm up to block the attack, but he was too far behind. The blade had already buried itself in the soft tissue of his throat, then cut out through his trachea with a violent twisting motion. Roy's hand moved to the side of his neck, touching it then looking at his blood covered palm in shock.

Krystal's training kicked in as she pressed her advantage. Every one of them had to die and die fast if she was going to survive. She was methodical, calculating, and merciless in her assault, but it was fueled by a holy indignation.

Lenny and Richie couldn't believe what they were seeing.

Before they could react, Krystal stabbed Roy all over as fast as she could raise the knife, pick a target, and plunge it down again. She palmed his face with her free hand, keeping his upper body pushed back on his haunches, effectively trapping him in an awkward kneeling position. Roy was forced to support himself with one hand while the other attempted to stop her repeated efforts to kill him. When he blocked one area, something else was left vulnerable and she changed targets in a fraction of a second, continuing her onslaught as she shifted side to side, stabbing him over and over, shouting at the top of her lungs.

"DIE! DIE! DIE! DIE, YOU MOTHERFUCKER! DIE!"

Neck, heart, lungs, abdomen, groin. Blood spurted and poured and she kept on stabbing. When Roy tried to restrain her hand, she cut his tendons and stabbed him in another vital area.

Shaking off their disbelief, at last, Lenny and Richie took off toward Krystal. She circled around to Roy's back, using him as a shield while she stabbed over his shoulders into both clavicle wells.

When Lenny reached for her she flickered the blade out, plucking at an eyeball with the tip of the knife. It raked through the soft tissue, laying it open. Lenny screamed and turned away, dropping to the ground on his knees as both hands rose to cover his eye. A viscous fluid began flowing in between his fingers a mere moment later.

Richie tried to shoot around Roy and get Krystal before she could slip away, but it was to no avail. As he reached for her, she slashed across his lower forearm, the blade laying it wide open. He jerked it back as if touching a hot stove eye. Krystal thrust the knife into his carotid artery before he could block it then lunged backward to make sure he couldn't grab her.

Krystal circled away to keep Roy in between them while she watched both Roy and Richie's injuries spurt blood like geysers.

Richie clamped a hand over his wound, but it was no use. The blood was pumping out fast. Roy was an even more hopeless cause. He had so many holes in his bucket, he was pretty much like a sprinkler at this point. Blood was bursting out of him all over, running like a multitude of rivers.

Lenny stumbled and fell against the brick wall, several feet away from Krystal. Krystal moved in front of Roy again and squatted down at eye level with him.

"*FUUUUUUCK!!! YOUUUUU!!!*" she yelled with every ounce of animosity she had pent up inside her, then spit in Roy's face. "Fuck you, you racist motherfucker!!"

She held the blade up, point aimed at his face.

"You fucking loser!" Krystal grinned big and flickered out a quick stab to his left eye. Roy's head flinched away, a gurgling roar of pain trying to make its way out of his mouth. She stabbed him again in the throat. "Beat by the black girl!" In the heart. "Loser!" she screamed in his face. "You're a fucking loser!" The stabs came rapid fire then, her hand cycling on a short path, in and out, over and over.

Roy's body began to topple to one side as he lost consciousness. Krystal released him and he ended up face down, fading, destined to wake up in hell if there truly was one -- and Krystal prayed there was. This brief moment of pain was not enough punishment. It could never be enough.

She glanced over at Richie in time to see him collapse against the wall and slide down to the ground in a limp mass, his constitution not nearly as vigorous as Roy's.

"You fucking bitch whore!" Lenny kept shouting, not knowing exactly where Krystal was. "You stabbed me in the eye! You fucking black cunt! I'm glad we killed your husband … *your kid* … I'm glad Roy raped your whore ass too! Fuck you!"

THUNK!

The blade drove down into his right clavicle well, severing the subclavian artery.

"No…" Krystal whispered into Lenny's ear. "Fuck you, you *ignorant fucking* bastard."

She ratcheted the blade back and forth with sharp, jerking movements to make sure it did sufficient damage to kill him, then she shoved Lenny to the floor to watch him as he began bleeding out.

It wasn't enough.

A flaming fury burned within Krystal. It embraced her whole being with a rage so intense, its light alone held the darkness at bay … the darkness where grief, despair and absolute misery lay in wait for her, their ambush inescapable. Wrath overcame her, but she didn't care. She gave in, becoming a channel for the hate she felt toward these men who had robbed her today of all that she valued. Krystal's fists clenched so tight her whole upper body trembled and shook. Her jaws clamped down, neck muscles rigid. Air whistled in between her teeth as she breathed in and out, inhaling and exhaling in sharp bursts.

"You fucking pieces of shit!" she screamed at last. "You *stupid, fucking, morons*!" Each word was punctuated by a soccer kick to Lenny's ribcage. He was the only one left alive, the only one she could make feel some small portion of her pain before he escaped her vengeance. He groaned and coughed up blood, his left hand pressed against the knife wound.

"Why?" she shrieked with each kick now. "Why? Why? Why?"

Adrenaline made her breathing uncontrolled. She panted for more oxygen.

"Why did you have to steal my baby!?" Krystal's left hand gripped the shirt material over her heart and twisted it. "My husband?"

She sobbed violently now, chest heaving, body bowing, unable to stand upright.

"Stupid! Stupid! Stupid! *Fucking hell*, it's all so pointless! *Pointless!* All for nothing! Nothing! You fucking piece of shit! *NOTHING!!*

She dropped to her knees, plunging the blade into Lenny's chest. He gasped but was too near death to resist as her blade rose and fell again, cycling up and down with blinding speed, Krystal's ferocity on full display as her blade ripped through Lenny's torso, each stab making a faint sound as she drove it through his clothing and into his flesh, then quickly pulled the knife back out to do it again.

SHICK! SHICK! SHICK! SHICK! SHICK! SHICK! SHICK! SHICK! SHICK! SHICK!

It was cathartic, like a volcanic eruption, but the lava never stopped flowing.

Krystal stopped, realizing at last Lenny was good and dead. Sitting back on her ankles, she stared at the scene for some time, wishing there was still someone else alive to stab or kick… repeatedly.

After several minutes of vacant fixation without active thought, she stooped to pull the shirt off of Richie's dead body. She took it and swaddled Matthew's head with the bloody fabric, hiding the brutal injuries she did not want to see. Once done, she lifted him gently, cradling her lifeless boy in both arms, then began walking back out to the street.

Krystal's life was upended and overturned, eviscerated of any hope and stuffed full of futility. In the time it would normally take her to drive to work or stop in at the grocery store for a small shopping trip or take a bubble bath, her world had been destroyed, razed to the ground. The gravity of her circumstances was boundless, each step heavier than the last. An exponentially increasing dread dragged her down with inexorable force. Krystal's sheer will alone fueled every ounce of effort as she strained to put one foot in front of the other.

*****

Five hundred and forty-three. That's how many steps it took for Krystal to make her way back to the crime scene where Officer Santiago was murdered by Roy. She counted each shuffle forward, no matter how minimal the movement, her short footsteps like those of a man condemned to walk the plank at sea.

"Mary, mother of God."

A rookie police officer standing guard at the crime scene perimeter blurted out when he saw Krystal headed his way, the rag doll limp body of a dead child in her arms.

He grabbed his radio mic and keyed it.

"Dispatch, this is 2088."

"Go ahead 2088," Dispatch responded.

"Dispatch, I need EMS to respond to the south perimeter wall of this investigation I'm on. I have a black female in her mid-twenties approaching me right now. She's carrying a child who appears to be either seriously injured or possibly DOA."

"Copy that 2088. I'll get EMS in route as soon as I can free someone up."

He walked forward, meeting Krystal as she crossed the street, thousand-yard stare looking right past him until he was mere feet away and standing right in front of her.

The first thing O'Brien noticed was the little arms, dangling limp and streaked with trails of dried blood which were, no doubt, dripping just minutes before.

"Ma'am," he greeted her, "I'm Officer O'Brien. I have EMS in route. What's wrong with your child?"

Krystal remained silent as she held out Matthew for him to take. It was then O'Brian noticed the blood-soaked shirt wrapped about Matthew's head, covering his face in its entirety, the wet material conforming to his face, except it didn't hold the form of a face any longer.

O'Brien took the child's body in his arms. He had no doubt the child was dead but he checked for a pulse anyway. Nothing. He didn't want to see this child's bloody and disfigured face but he needed to provide CPR if possible. He unwrapped the shirt from around the skull and blanched white at the sight. There wasn't a nose or mouth present to give breaths into. He laid the shirt back over the child's face.

O'Brien breathed deep before looking into Krystal's vacant eyes.

"What's…" he started and had to swallow hard to prevent himself from crying before speaking again. "What's your child's name, ma'am?" he asked.

Krystal was mute and possibly deaf and blind as well. She offered no answer, no response of any kind. After some seconds, O'Brien spoke again, his tone gentle and calm.

"Ma'am? Can you hear me?" he asked.

Krystal was still non-responsive. Officer O'Brien shifted Matthew's body to his chest, holding him with one arm, then stepped forward and turned to stand next to her and placed his free hand on Krystal's upper back.

"Ma'am."

"Matthew," she whispered.

"Matthew," O'Brien parroted back to her. He used his hand to guide her over to the side of the street where he helped her sit down on the curb. He took a seat next to her, holding Matthew and making sure she was not alone while they waited for EMS to arrive.

He cradled Matthew in his left arm while he applied compressions to the boy's sternum with his right hand. O'Brien knew he couldn't declare the child dead. He had to perform CPR of some sort until EMS arrived.

"Do you have a husband?" he inquired, his palm pushing down and lifting up at a steady pace. "Can we contact him for you?"

"Dead," Krystal answered, her heart bled of all emotion for the moment.

"OK," O'Brien responded. "Um, did he die today along with your son or some time ago?"

"Today," she said. "He was murdered… Nazis."

"Did they hurt your son also?"

Krystal nodded her head.

"Do you know who they are?"

Krystal nodded her head again.

"How about where they are, ma'am?"

"Dead," she said, her face expressing satisfaction for a moment. "I killed them. All three of them," she confessed. "They're in the alley over there that leads to the back of that old funeral home." Krystal pointed without looking as she said: "over there."

O'Brien couldn't believe what he was hearing. He did not think this young lady capable of killing three people, even if it was self-defense. They sat in silence the rest of the time while they waited to hear the approaching sirens. Krystal's anger bled out and despair swept in. She couldn't think a coherent thought, much less speak and answer questions.

She's in shock, O'Brien thought. *Might as well be a deaf-mute right now.*

An EMS medic named Jane took Matthew's body into the ambulance to confirm what they already knew. Another, Randy, assessed Krystal, asking O'Brien questions when he realized Krystal wasn't going to be answering them any time soon.

At some point Jane opened the door and made eye contact with O'Brien, shaking her head back in forth, tears rolling down her cheeks.

Once Randy determined Krystal was in no immediate physical danger they loaded her up for transport to the hospital. O'Brien followed behind the ambulance. It drove along, in no rush, obeying the speed limit, red lights flashing but no siren wailing.

At the hospital, the attending doctor determined that Krystal had been raped and collected evidence for the police investigation. While O'Brien waited for the evidence, Detective Sergeant Richards arrived. O'Brien filled him in on the known details then posed the question burning in his head to the senior officer.

"She confessed to killing three white supremacists, sir. Are we going to arrest her?"

O'Brien looked sick at the very idea, but he wasn't sure. He had heard some horror stories from other cops about people protecting themselves getting locked up in prison.

"You fucking shitting me, kid?" the detective blurted out. "She deserves a fucking medal if you ask me." The detective sat down in the chair next to O'Brien. "But…" he continued, "it's ultimately up to the District Attorney. He has the final say. But hell! What jury would convict this lady, given the circumstances?"

O'Brien breathed a sigh of relief.

"I'm going to check in on her before I stand relieved, sir," he advised the detective.

Richards nodded his head.

O'Brien walked into the ER and found Krystal's curtained room. He stood at the foot of the bed until she acknowledged his presence.

"Hi. A detective is here to speak to you when you're ready. I'm leaving, but if you need anything, feel free to contact me."

O'Brien laid the business card on her upper thighs when she didn't extend a hand.

"I'm so sorry for your loss, ma'am… I truly am, but, one word of advice."

O'Brien paused and squatted down at the end of the bed, bringing his eyes in line with her gaze. After several seconds, her eyes shifted to actively look at him.

"Lawyer," he said. "Lawyer. I doubt you'll get charged or anything, but before you give a statement, have a lawyer present."

O'Brien tapped the foot of her bed as he stood, nodded his head at her and walked away.

Krystal sat propped up, TV droning in her left ear from the tethered remote speaker, but none of it registering on her brain.

She shut her eyes tight and pleaded with God above that when she opened them she would be in her chair on the beach. She would look out over the waves and see Kendall and Matthew playing in the surf or building their sand castle. To think otherwise was too much. Too much for her heart to bear. This knowledge of evil committed against her, the theft of husband and child, threatened her sanity.

Denial was the only relief she could find.

It can't be true, she thought, eyes remaining closed. *It has to be a nightmare.*

N*ot* a wife. N*ot* a mother. This reality was inconceivable. Sure, she had prepared herself for years to deal with the potential that Kendall could die in combat, but not like this, and she certainly never considered Matthew's death as even a remote possibility.

This can't be my life. It just can't be.

Krystal opened her eyes and instead of a beach chair, she still lay on the hospital gurney, curtain drawn. A man in khaki slacks and a dark blue sports jacket stood there, notepad in hand, staring at her.

"Hi, Mrs. Pittman. Detective Sergeant Richards. I knocked and called but you didn't answer. Once I saw you sitting there like that I didn't want to interrupt you. Can we talk?"

An elephant might as well have eased itself down onto Krystal's chest, breaking her ribs in slow motion, the bony fragments piercing her heart in multiplicity. With each beat, hope drained out from every torn chamber.

She tried to speak but the words stuck in her constricting throat. She gulped hard, trying to swallow, but the spit had dried inside her mouth. With immense effort, she managed to croak out a simple demand.

"Tell me… tell me what happened… to my boys…"

She locked her eyes with his, demanding a verdict she did not want to hear but desperately needed someone to speak. Speak the words and make it real, undeniable. Like a mountainous boulder blocking a road, she could *never, ever* travel again.

Richards shuffled his feet and looked down, appearing uncomfortable with her gaze, a window thrown wide on the stark anguish filling Krystal's soul. After a deep breath, he stood erect and looked into her eyes.

"Mrs. Pittman …" he paused.

"Tell me …" she groaned, her voice cracking.

Richards nodded.

"OK. Mrs. Pittman, your husband was killed earlier this afternoon by a group of white supremacists. After that, they tracked you down, killed your son, and raped you. Somehow you managed to defend yourself, killing three of them with a knife. Afterward, you found Officer O'Brien, who helped bring you here to the hospital, where the doctor confirmed that you were indeed raped and collected evidence to support his conclusions."

Richards stopped there to let Krystal process what he had said.

Her eyes welled with tears. Her face began to screw itself into a twisted mask of agonizing dread.

"My boys … are dead?" her voice creaked, the pitch was so high.

Richards' lips pressed together into a thin line. It broke his heart to deliver this kind of news, but it was especially troubling when the person remained reluctant to accept the truth and he had to repeat it in an effort to convince them.

"Yes, Mrs. Pittman. I'm sorry, but both your boys are dead."

Her eyes squeezed shut and tears flowed down her cheeks, dropping onto the white sheets. The dam burst, her chest heaved, and violent sobs wracked her body without any sign of restraint. Krystal covered her face with both hands, and lay back, curling into the fetal position. A bleating wail bled out of her lungs, filling the entire ER, as something inside her finally gave up the ghost and died.

Despair smothered her ability to breathe by degrees, each inhalation more labored than the last. Suffocating. The desolation she felt at their loss was suffocating, the pain a paralytic poison condemning her to death with them, except she'd still be here, an empty shell, a shadow of her once joyful self.

I can't live like this, her mind screamed.

Her entire world was undone. The heavens burned, the seas boiled, the mountains heaved from their foundations. There was nowhere safe for her in this apocalyptic aftermath of hate. Everything she was lay in ruin, gutted of any beauty, broken, dysfunctional.

Krystal felt around with one hand for the call button. She needed a sedative, needed to sleep, turn off her brain, turn off the wrenching pain in her heart… but she couldn't stop weeping long enough to form words. Her brain scrambled for a solution, a way to manage this whirlwind of relentless pain forcing her diaphragm to contract and expand like some blacksmith's bellows, fanning a fire that would never die, a blazing black darkness sent to drown the light of life and devastate her sanity. A maddening, deep, deep hole that would swaddle her in pitch and whisper "vanity of vanities, meaningless, meaningless, everything is meaningless," no matter how much she offered supplication to the universe for a 'why'.

Indignation.

She remembered how her unrestrained anger held this abyssal depression at bay earlier.

Embrace the wrath. Embrace hate…

She considered the irony, for a brief moment, but decided she didn't care. Her hate would be the product of righteous conviction, a sweet flower sprung from the blood of her lost family.

Just.

Her hate would be justified, and it would secure the reparations due to her. Krystal dragged Roy and his boys into her mind's eye, focusing on them, visualizing what they did to her son, to her. A moment of anger flashed bright, like a spark trying to light a fire, but the tinder was damp with tears. It didn't kindle. It didn't blaze. Instead, it began to sputter and die.

They're not enough, she confided to herself after much effort. *I killed them. There's nothing tangible left to pursue, to harm. The anger will not hold. The rage will not last.*

In her mind, she began reliving every horrible thing which had befallen her earlier in the day, but in reverse. One moment at a time she worked backward, looking at every detail she could remember until she stumbled onto a truth she could seize upon.

"Those two, big Antifa fuckers," Krystal mumbled aloud.

"Excuse me?" Richards inquired. "What did you say, Mrs. Pittman?" He put pen to paper in his notebook and awaited her response.

Krystal pushed herself into an upright position. Richards grabbed a handful of tissues from the counter and handed them to her. Krystal took them and divided their use between wiping her eyes and blowing her nose. When she looked up, her composure had undergone an uncanny transformation. Her expression was cold and measured, but an unquenchable rage smoldered in her eyes.

Richards recognized the look. He'd seen it in the mirror before.

"You were saying, Mrs. Pittman?"

Krystal placed her hands in her lap and spoke.

"Two big fat fucks with the Antifa group. It's all their fault. If they hadn't started shit with Kendall and punched me in the face, we wouldn't have been running from them in the car. If we hadn't been running from them in the car, Kendall wouldn't have ended up plowing into the white supremacist crowd and putting a huge target on our backs."

Richards nodded, seeming to agree with her summation of events.

"Is there anything you can tell me about these two fellas? Any physical description? Names? Anything?"

Krystal stared off into space, her brain searching for whatever details she could recall. Her breathing slowed. The pressure in her center lifted. The gnawing pain in her soul lost its edge, hate distracting her from the worst of it.

In her mind, she could see them both clear as crystal.

"They both looked a lot like that rapper Biggie Smalls. About the same size and build. I could only see part of their faces. They were wearing bandannas."

Richards waited a few seconds before prompting Krystal.

"Anything else that would help me identify them?"

Krystal searched her memories, envisioning the scene while trying to recall all the smells and sounds she might have picked up on.

Jerry, she remembered. *The one who hit me, his name was Jerry.*

She opened her mouth to speak and stopped herself.

I can find him. I'm sure of it. I don't need the police. I can make him pay. Make him talk. And when he tells me the other fucker's name, I can make him pay too.

"Mrs. Pittman? You were about to say something?" Richards asked.

Krystal's heart burned bright with anger. Like a dying man raging against the coming night, she would hold back the tide of despair with a spiteful fury. A guiltless malevolence animated her entire being.

"No, sir, detective," she answered him, shaking her head side to side. "Not a thing."

Richards looked at her, eyes narrowing in distrust.

"OK, then," he enunciated in a deliberate manner, "how 'bout you tell me what happened with the three white supremacists we found dead in the back-alley entrance to the old funeral home? What did you have to do to protect yourself?"

Krystal's eyes narrowed as well, recognizing the shift in Richards' demeanor.

He knows I'm hiding something.

"Detective Richards," Krystal addressed him formally, her countenance full of sincerity. "I only have one thing to say about all that."

She paused, waiting for him to ask. Richards bit to move things along.

"What would that be?" he asked.

"Lawyer."

Krystal leaned her head back against the pillow and closed her eyes, fingers clenching tight, nails biting into her palm, almost as if the blade was already in her hand and at Jerry's throat.

The End

Made in the USA
Middletown, DE
01 November 2018